NANCY DREW

#22 AND THE CLUE CREW

Unicorn Uproar

BY CAROLYN KEENE

ILLUSTRATED BY MACKY PAMINTUAN

Aladdin

New York London Toronto Sydney

⬥ ALADDIN
An imprint of Simon & Schuster Children's Publishing Division
1230 Avenue of the Americas, New York, NY 10020
First Aladdin paperback edition September 2009
Text copyright © 2009 by Simon & Schuster, Inc.
Illustrations copyright © 2009 by Macky Pamintuan
All rights reserved, including the right of reproduction in whole or in part in any form.
ALADDIN is a trademark of Simon & Schuster, Inc., and related logo is a registered trademark of Simon & Schuster, Inc.
NANCY DREW and related logos are registered trademarks of Simon & Schuster, Inc.
NANCY DREW AND THE CLUE CREW is a registered trademark of Simon & Schuster, Inc.
For information about special discounts for bulk purchases, please contact Simon & Schuster Special Sales at 1-866-506-1949 or business@simonandschuster.com.
The Simon & Schuster Speakers Bureau can bring authors to your live event. For more information or to book an event contact the Simon & Schuster Speakers Bureau at 1-866-248-3049 or visit our website at www.simonspeakers.com.
Designed by Lisa Vega
The text of this book was set in ITC Stone Informal.
Manufactured in the United States of America
10 9 8 7 6 5 4 3 2 1
Library of Congress Control Number 2008942951
ISBN 978-1-4169-7810-7
ISBN 978-1-4169-9653-8 (eBook)

CONTENTS

ChaPTER ONE

Medieval Magic

"Good people of River Heights!" Mayor Strong announced. His suit of armor creaked as he threw his arms up into the air. "I, Sir Mayor the Strong, welcome thee to the Dragon's Breath Fair!"

Eight-year-old Nancy Drew cheered with her best friends, Bess Marvin and George Fayne. It was the start of the Dragon's Breath Fair, a medieval festival that came to the girls' town every fall.

"What is 'medieval,' anyway?" Bess asked.

"It was a time hundreds of years ago," Nancy explained. "When there were kings, queens, jesters—and knights in shining armor."

"And dragons!" George said, her dark eyes

flashing. "Don't forget about dragons."

"Oh, no!" Bess gasped. "What do we do if we run into a fire-breathing dragon here at the fair?"

"Roast marshmallows!" George joked.

The girls turned back to the mayor. He was telling the crowd the fun they would have.

"There will be jugglers, games, hearty food, and puppet shows," Mayor Strong boomed. "And the most thrilling challenge of all—the joust!"

"I know what a joust is," George said to Nancy and Bess. "It's when two knights on horseback try to knock weapons out of each other's hands."

"Of course, I would love to be in the joust myself," Mayor Strong told everyone. "But first I need a horse!"

The visor on the mayor's helmet fell in front of his face with a *clunk*.

"He needs a horse *and* a new helmet," George whispered.

The mayor raised his visor and shouted, "I hereby declare the Dragon's Breath Fair open!"

After a big cheer the crowd scattered in all

directions into the fairgrounds. Nancy didn't know what was more colorful, the striped tents and banners hanging everywhere, or the red, yellow, and gold leaves on the trees.

"Do you think they had detectives in those days?" Bess asked. "Detectives like us?"

Nancy smiled at the thought. She, Bess, and George were good at solving mysteries. So good that they'd started their own detective club called the Clue Crew.

"Sure, they had detectives," Nancy decided. "Somebody had to figure out who stole the queen of hearts's tarts!"

"And speaking of stuff that's yummy for the tummy," George said, nodding in the direction of the food stalls, "there's my mom."

Nancy could see Mrs. Fayne stacking jumbo cookies on the ledge of a food stall. Mrs. Fayne ran her own catering company and was in charge of the food at the Dragon's Breath Fair. She was also in charge of bringing Nancy, Bess, and George to the fair every day that weekend.

"What should we do first?" Bess asked, rubbing her hands together. "Play a game or eat one of those cookies?"

Nancy wanted to watch the archery contest—until she noticed a wooden sign stuck in the ground. It had a red arrow and the words THIS WAY TO WIZARDLY WOODS.

"What's Wizardly Woods?" Nancy wondered.

"There's only one way to find out," George said.

The girls followed the path until they reached more colorful tents, their flaps wide open. Inside were men and women selling jewelry, candles, and scented oils. Outside a blue tent decorated with silver stars stood a rack holding dried flower garlands.

Bess grabbed a garland and placed it over her long blond hair. "Does this make me look princessy?" she asked.

"You mean *prissy*!" George said, and smirked.

"Very funny, *Georgia*," Bess replied, and smirked back. "Sometimes I can't believe we're cousins!"

George gritted her teeth. She hated her real

name, Georgia, even more than she hated wearing dresses and skirts—a major difference between Bess and George.

Bess was about to look for a mirror when a voice called out: "Huzzah, fair maidens! Do you like magic?"

Nancy turned to see a woman wearing hoop earrings and a tunic decorated with stars.

"You mean like card tricks?" George asked.

"Cards are for playing Fish," the woman scoffed. "But if it's magic you're looking for, Enchanted Elly has just the thing for you!"

Out from behind her back Enchanted Elly pulled a magic wand. Lavender ribbons streamed from the long silver stick. But the best part was the glittery purple star on top.

"It's awesome!" Nancy exclaimed.

"And it can be yours for a mere pittance," Elly said.

"A what?" Nancy asked, scrunching her nose.

"That's medieval for five dollars," Elly said. She nodded at the flower garlands on the rack.

"I'll even throw three garlands into the deal."

"Buy it, Nancy," George whispered. "You love purple!"

"And I love this garland!" Bess said, patting her head.

"So what do you say, Red?" Elly asked, nodding at Nancy.

Nancy knew Elly was talking to her because she had reddish-blond hair. She also knew she wanted that magic wand more than anything.

"I say yes!" Nancy said, digging into her jacket pocket for a five-dollar bill. "I'll take it!"

"Is it really magic?" George asked Elly. "I mean, does it come with a spell book or something?"

"You make up the spells," Elly explained. She raised the wand into the air. "Then you just point—and poof!"

Elly handed Nancy the magic wand. Then she selected garlands, which she placed over Nancy's and George's heads.

"There, m'ladies!" Elly declared. "Now beauty will follow you wherever you go."

"You mean bees will follow us!" George groaned, looking up at the dried flowers encircling her dark curls.

As the girls left the Wizardly Woods, Nancy couldn't take her eyes off her new wand. She waved it in the air, making the lavender ribbons twirl.

"Ohmigosh," Bess gasped. "I never saw any-thing so amazing!"

"Thanks," Nancy said, still gazing at her wand.

"No, not your wand, Nancy," Bess said. She pointed into the distance. "That!"

Nancy looked to see where Bess was pointing. Then she gasped too.

Inside a fenced-in pen was a magnificent white creature with a mane and tail like a horse. But a single silver horn on the creature's head told Nancy it wasn't a horse at all. It was—

"A unicorn!" Nancy cried.

CHaPTER TWO

Spells Bells

The girls raced to the fence. The unicorn stood at the far end of the pen, too far away for them to get a good look.

"My mom said there would be a unicorn here at the fair," George said. "But I thought she was joking!"

"That's no joke," Bess said, staring over the fence at the unicorn. "That's got to be for real."

Until now Nancy had seen unicorns only in books and as stuffed animals in toy stores. But the unicorn inside the pen looked pretty for-real to her.

"The sign says his name is Sparkle," Nancy pointed out.

"Probably because his horn sparkles in the sun!" Bess declared.

The girls were about to call out to Sparkle when a jingly noise made them turn around. Nancy giggled when she saw Toby Leo from their third-grade class walking over. He was wearing a floppy jester's cap with tiny gold bells sewed to the ends!

"Are you supposed to be a jester, Toby?" Nancy asked.

"What did you think I was?" Toby said, shaking his head to jingle his bells. "The Mr. Drippy ice cream truck?"

"Ha, ha, very funny," Bess said.

"Funny is right!" Toby said. "Jesters used to tell jokes to the king and queen. Do you want to hear a joke?"

"Go for it," George said with a shrug.

"Okay," Toby said. He stuck

out his hand. "That'll cost you a dollar."

Nancy groaned under her breath. Toby Leo was always looking for ways to earn a buck.

"Come on," Toby urged. "Cough it up."

"Why should we pay you for a joke?" Nancy asked. "George tells great jokes, and they don't cost a penny."

"Then tell me one," Toby told George.

"Sure," George said. She stuck out her own hand. "But that'll cost you *two* dollars!"

Toby smirked as if to say *Ha, ha*. Then he pointed over the fence and said, "What's that thing with the crazy horn on its head? Some kind of ringtoss game?"

"It's not a ringtoss game," Bess said. "It's a unicorn!"

"A what-a-corn?" Toby asked.

"Unicorn," Bess repeated. "I once read that unicorns are magical, can leap over rainbows, and are good luck—if you can catch one."

"Good luck, huh?" Toby asked slowly. His eyes

lit up as he stared at Sparkle. "Now, *that* gives me an idea!"

The girls watched as Toby dashed away.

"What kind of idea do you think he meant?" Nancy asked.

"Maybe an idea for a unicorn joke," George said. "Like, why did the unicorn try out for the school band?"

"Why?" Nancy and Bess asked together.

"Because he had his own horn!" George declared, sending the girls into a fit of giggles.

Nancy, Bess, and George were about to turn back to Sparkle when a girl wearing a long princess dress raced over. She pointed over the fence at Sparkle and cried, "There, Daddy! I want that for my Totally Tubular Tenth Birthday Party!"

"Isn't that Destiny Delgado from the fifth grade?" Nancy whispered.

"It's her, all right," George whispered back. "I heard Destiny's parents are so rich they eat off of gold plates!"

"I heard the only reason Destiny doesn't go

to private school is because she hates the uniforms," Bess whispered.

Mr. Delgado joined Destiny at the fence. So did another man dressed in a green tunic and matching tights.

"Who's that? Robin Hood?" Bess asked.

"That's Rex Martindale, the director of the Dragon's Breath Fair," George said. "He came to our house to talk to my mom last week. But he wasn't dressed like that."

Destiny began jumping up and down. "Daddy!" she said. "Tell Rex I want that unicorn for my Totally Tubular Tenth Birthday Party!"

Mr. Delgado turned to Rex and said, "Destiny's birthday party will have a medieval theme. Just like here at the fair."

"Yes!" Destiny said. She flipped her hair over her shoulder. "I'll be the princess and all my friends will be the peasants."

"It's always been her dream," Mr. Delgado added.

Nancy rolled her eyes. Destiny didn't need a

medieval party to be a princess—she already was one!

"I'm sorry, Mr. Delgado," Rex said, sighing. "The unicorn is our main attraction. He has to stay here all weekend."

"It's not fair!" Destiny cried. "Daddy, do something!"

The girls stepped away from the fence.

"Destiny is spoiling our visit with Sparkle," Bess complained. "I wish she would just disappear or something."

"Did you say disappear?" Nancy asked, and giggled. She pointed her wand straight at Destiny. Then in a low voice said, "Abracadabra, abraca-dear. Make Destiny disappear!"

"Nancy, don't!" Bess gasped.

"Don't worry, Bess," Nancy said. "Destiny is still there. That means my wand isn't really magic. Just pretty."

"Yeah, pretty *scary*," Bess said, and shuddered.

A woman dressed in a red cape and feathered cap shouted as she walked by: "Lords and ladies, boys and girls! Come one, come all to ye royal parade!"

"Let's go," Nancy said. She stuck her wand into the back pocket of her jeans. Then she ran with Bess and George to catch the parade.

A crowd had already gathered on the field for the parade. Nancy, Bess, and George squeezed to the front just in time to see marching knights, jugglers, and the king and queen waving from a castle float.

When Nancy spotted Enchanted Elly marching in the parade, she remembered her magic wand. But when she glanced back at her pocket, it was gone.

"Bess, George!" Nancy cried. "I think I lost my wand!"

"Maybe it really was magic," Bess gasped. "And it magically disappeared!"

George shook her head and said, "Or maybe it just fell out of your pocket on the way here."

The girls left the parade to retrace their steps. As they neared Sparkle's pen, Nancy spotted a flash of silver in the grass. As they ran closer, the glittery purple star and lavender ribbons came into view.

Nancy smiled with relief as she picked up the wand. "See, Bess?" she said happily. "It didn't disappear."

But Bess wasn't looking at the wand. She was staring into the unicorn pen.

"You guys . . . what happened to Sparkle?" Bess asked.

"What do you mean?" Nancy asked. She looked into Sparkle's pen too. But instead of seeing the white unicorn, she saw Rex Martindale. His hands were on his hips as he spoke loudly to a teenage boy.

"Seth, as Sparkle's handler you should know where he is!" Rex was saying.

"I told you, Rex," Seth said. "When I got back to the pen, Sparkle was gone."

Nancy, Bess, and George traded stunned looks.

"Did he say Sparkle was gone?" Nancy whispered. "As in . . . missing?"

Chapter Three

Point and Poof

"He can't be gone!" Bess cried. "We never got a chance to pet him. Or watch him jump over a rainbow!"

"Let's see what we can find out," Nancy whispered.

The three girls inched closer toward the pen. Rex and Seth were so busy arguing that they didn't notice the girls.

"Where were you all this time, Seth?" Rex asked.

"I left Sparkle to help Mayor Strong," Seth answered. "He said it was important—"

"What could be more important than our

main attraction?" Rex cut in. "Maybe you left the gate open!"

"When I came back, the gate was latched," Seth said. "Sparkle must have found some other way to get out."

"I don't care how he got out," Rex huffed. "Just call me the second you find him."

"Why don't I call the police in the meantime?" Seth suggested. "Maybe they can look for Sparkle."

"Not the police!" Rex cried. "If our guests see the police, they'll know something is wrong."

"But—," Seth started to say.

"Sparkle will come back when he's hungry," Rex cut in. "In the meantime let's take that sign down so people won't look for a unicorn in here."

Rex and Seth left the pen, not bothering to lock the gate. After Rex pulled the sign out of the ground, the two walked right past the girls in the direction of the parade.

"If that guy Seth said the gate was latched," George wondered out loud, "how could Sparkle have gotten out?"

"Maybe Nancy's magic wand made Sparkle disappear," Bess said.

"My wand?" Nancy cried.

"Enchanted Elly said you just point and poof," Bess explained. "Maybe you pointed your wand at Destiny but poofed Sparkle by mistake."

Nancy glanced at her wand. She shook her head and said, "Sparkle was still in his pen after I waved my wand. You waved good-bye to him, remember?"

"Some spells might take longer to work," George said.

Nancy couldn't believe her ears. Now both her best friends were blaming her wand!

"There's got to be a reason Sparkle isn't in his pen," Nancy said. "And we're going to find out why."

"You mean as the Clue Crew?" Bess asked.

"Here?" George said. "At a medieval fair?"

"Sure," Nancy said, smiling. "Finding a missing unicorn is more important than finding the queen's tarts!"

The girls walked through the gate into Sparkle's pen. Nancy found hundreds of hoofprints in the mud-packed ground. Bess found something too—a tiny golden bell!

"Where did this come from?" Bess asked. She held it up and gave it a jingle. The sound made Nancy think of Toby.

"Toby was wearing bells on his jester's cap,"

Nancy pointed out. "Maybe he was here inside the pen."

"Hey," George said, "maybe that idea Toby came up with was to steal Sparkle."

"Why would Toby steal a unicorn?" Bess asked.

"To sell!" George exclaimed. "If he could get a dollar for a dumb joke, think how much he could get for something magical that leaps over rainbows."

"He'd be richer than Destiny Delgado," Bess agreed.

"Destiny wanted a unicorn for her Totally Tubular Tenth Birthday Party," Nancy said excitedly. "And whatever Destiny wants, Destiny gets."

The girls had two suspects. But they needed more clues. As Nancy studied the hoofprints, something clicked.

"There are no hoofprints leading to the gate," Nancy pointed out. "So Sparkle couldn't have left through there."

"Sparkle is a unicorn," Bess stated. "If unicorns can leap over rainbows, they can leap over fences."

"Hey, you!" a voice called out.

Nancy, Bess, and George spun around. Standing outside the pen was Seth, Sparkle's handler.

"What are you doing?" Seth demanded. "You won't find anything in there."

"That's what he thinks," Bess whispered as she pocketed the tiny gold bell. "We already did."

"Did you plant tomatoes, Hannah?" Nancy asked. "You know how much I love tomatoes!"

It was late afternoon and Nancy was home from the fair. She carefully plucked a ripe tomato from Hannah's vegetable garden in the Drews' backyard. Hannah Gruen picked up something too—Nancy's wand. She pointed it at Nancy and said, "You wish for tomatoes? And so you shall have!"

"Hannah, don't!" Nancy gasped. "You might turn me into a tomato—or a toad!"

Hannah laughed as she placed the wand back on the picnic table. "Nancy, I've been your housekeeper since you were three years old," she teased. "If I wanted to turn you into a toad, I would have done it a long time ago."

Nancy knew that Hannah was a lot more than a housekeeper. Hannah loved Nancy almost as much as her mother once had, before she'd died. And she would never turn Nancy into a toad!

What was I thinking? Nancy thought glumly. *Now I'm starting to believe my wand is magic too!*

The phone rang inside the house.

"I'll get it, Hannah," Nancy said. "It might be Bess or George."

"Of course!" Hannah chuckled. "You haven't seen one another for two whole hours."

Nancy entered the kitchen through the back door. She picked up the phone and said, "Hello?"

"Is this Nancy?" a girl's voice asked. "Nancy Drew?"

Nancy frowned. The voice sounded shaky, as if the girl on the other end were worried.

"This is Nancy," Nancy said slowly.

"Good," the girl said. "Because I need your help and I need it now."

CHAPTER FOUR

Horseplay

"Who is this?" Nancy asked.

"Sophie Wang," the girl answered. "I go to your school. I'm in the fifth grade."

A fifth grader is calling me? Nancy thought excitedly. *Cool!*

"What's up, Sophie?" Nancy asked, trying not to sound too excited.

"I take horseback riding lessons at the River Heights Riding Academy," Sophie explained. "I'm going to be in a big horse show there next Saturday."

"Neat!" Nancy said.

"Not anymore," Sophie sighed. "The horse I

always ride at the academy has been missing for days."

"How do you know he's missing?" Nancy asked. "Did someone tell you he is?"

"Not really," Sophie said. "My instructor Matt just keeps telling me the same thing over and over again: 'Carrot Cake is unavailable right now.'"

"Did you ask him why?" Nancy asked.

"Every time I do, Matt changes the subject," Sophie said. "That's why I think something is wrong."

Nancy thought so too. Why wouldn't Matt tell Sophie what had happened to Carrot Cake unless it was something bad?

"I can ride a horse named Babe in the show," Sophie sighed. "But Babe doesn't jump as high as Carrot Cake. And she has the worst oat breath!"

"So . . . what do you want me to do?" Nancy asked.

"I've heard about the Clue Crew at school," Sophie explained. "I want you and your friends to

27

find Carrot Cake so I can ride him in the show."

"Really?" Nancy squeaked. A fifth grader wanted the Clue Crew's help? Wait until Bess and George heard!

But then Nancy remembered Sparkle. Solving two cases in one weekend would be too much—even for the Clue Crew.

"Well? Can you do it?" Sophie asked.

Nancy took a deep breath, then said, "Sorry, Sophie. But we can't."

"Why?" Sophie cried.

"Because we have to find a—" Nancy stopped mid-sentence. How could she tell a fifth grader they had to find a missing unicorn?

"Find a what?" Sophie asked.

"It's top secret," Nancy blurted. "Like all of the Clue Crew's cases."

"Please?" Sophie asked again. "I know you're only eight, but I heard you guys are smart for third graders."

Nancy wasn't sure if that was a compliment or an insult. But it didn't matter. They couldn't help Sophie find Carrot Cake. And that was that.

"Sorry, Sophie," Nancy said gently. "Maybe Carrot Cake is at the vet. Or at the blacksmith getting new shoes—"

CLICK.

Nancy hung up too. She saw her dog, Chocolate Chip, padding into the kitchen. Her Labrador puppy was holding her magic wand between her teeth.

Poor Sophie, Nancy thought as Chip chewed the wand on the kitchen floor. *But we have to find the missing unicorn first.*

Kneeling down, Nancy grabbed the wand from Chip's mouth. She held it up and sighed. "Before everybody blames this."

"You turned down a fifth grader?" George exclaimed the next morning. "This could have been huge!"

Nancy sat next to Bess and George in the backseat of Mrs. Fayne's van. They were headed for the second day of the Dragon's Breath Fair.

"We can't find a horse and a unicorn at the same time," Nancy insisted.

"But this Sophie was a fifth grader!" Bess cried. "We could have played with them at recess."

"Fifth graders get the best equipment at recess," George agreed.

"But third graders play better games," Nancy said. "And finding a missing unicorn is way cooler than finding a missing horse anyway."

"True, we have to find Sparkle before the fair ends tomorrow," Bess said. "And we only have two suspects: Toby and Destiny."

"Destiny's Totally Tubular Tenth Birthday Party is this afternoon at one o'clock," George informed them. "It said so on her blog."

"Destiny has her own blog?" Bess groaned. "Remind me never to read it."

"Okay, Clue Crew," Mrs. Fayne said, smiling into the rearview mirror. "Why don't you take a break from your case until we get to the fair?"

The girls decided to play a guessing game. They tried to guess what Mrs. Fayne was delivering to the festival by the smells inside the van.

"I smell hot dogs with mustard," Bess declared.

Nancy took a whiff and said, "Baked ziti."

"Toby Leo!" George shouted.

"You smell Toby Leo?" Bess cried.

"No!" George said, pointing out the van window. "I *see* Toby Leo right over there."

Nancy leaned over Bess and George to look out the window. Sure enough, Toby was walking his big sheepdog, Duncan, along River Street.

While Mrs. Fayne stopped for a red light, George rolled down the window and shouted, "Toby! Where are you going?"

Toby glanced sideways at the girls. Then without a word he began walking faster and faster. Duncan's shaggy white hair bounced as he hurried to keep up.

"Wait, Toby," Bess said. She held the little gold bell out the window. "Is this yours?"

But Toby and Duncan had already turned the corner.

"If Toby has a dog," Bess said, dropping the bell back into her pocket, "why would he want a unicorn, too?"

"Because he's allergic to cats?" George guessed.

"Well, we can't question Toby if he doesn't go to the fair today," Bess said.

"Destiny is a suspect too," Nancy said in a low voice. "We have to find a way to go to her party today."

"You mean her tenth birthday party?" Bess asked. "That would be totally . . . tubular!"

Mrs. Fayne drove the van onto the fairgrounds. Nancy, Bess, and George helped Mrs. Fayne carry some light boxes to the food stalls.

"Thanks, girls," Mrs. Fayne said after they were finished. "Why don't you go watch the joust now? I think it starts in a few minutes."

The girls had no trouble finding the jousting field. It was already filled with people climbing onto the bleachers.

"Look," George said, pointing, "there's Mayor Strong. I mean—Sir Mayor the Strong."

Helping Mayor Strong onto a horse was Seth. Once up, the mayor toppled back and forth in his bulky armor.

"I guess the mayor found a horse," Bess said.

The horse was wearing a tall feathery head-dress. Draped over his body was a thick blanket decorated with colorful crests. His legs, tail, and mane were snowy white.

That horse is as white as Sparkle, Nancy told herself. She bit her lower lip as another thought flashed into her head. *Unless . . . that horse is Sparkle!*

Nancy turned to her friends. "Mayor Strong needed a horse to be in the joust, right?" she asked.

"Right," Bess said with a nod.

"So," Nancy said with a grin. "What if Mayor Strong's horse is really a *unicorn*?"

CHAPTER FIVE

Sparkle or Speckle?

"How could that horse be a unicorn?" Bess asked. "Unicorns have horns on their heads."

"Look at the huge headdress the horse is wearing," Nancy pointed out. "His horn could be hidden underneath."

"If it is Sparkle," George said, tilting her head to study the horse, "how did the mayor get him?"

"Seth said he was helping Mayor Strong at the time Sparkle went missing," Nancy said. "Maybe he was helping the mayor get Sparkle!"

"But why would Mayor Strong want a unicorn instead of a horse?" Bess asked.

"Why not?" George said. "If unicorns jump superhigh, maybe they can run superfast, too!"

35

Seth led Mayor Strong and the mystery horse onto the jousting field.

"If we could only look under that headdress to see if there's a horn," Nancy said softly.

Three men wearing blue velvet tunics and tights walked to the middle of the field. They blew loudly into long skinny trumpets.

"Hear ye, hear ye, good people!" one man announced. "Challenging Sir Mayor the Strong in the royal joust shall be Sir Bragalot the Bold!"

Another knight in armor rode onto the field.

He was riding a black horse that was also wearing a headdress and blanket.

"Sir Bragalot rides the brave and noble mare Midnight," the man went on. "Sir Mayor the Strong will ride the gallant steed Speckle!"

"Speckle?" Nancy repeated.

"Speckle . . . Sparkle?" Bess said. She narrowed her eyes. "A coincidence? I think not."

"Brave knights, take thy places," the man shouted. "And may the joust begin!"

Both knights lowered their visors. They trotted

their horses to the opposite ends of the arena.

The knights then took pointed lances and shields from the horses' handlers. Mayor Strong had trouble holding both, and he dropped his shield on Seth's foot.

"This is going to be dangerous," Bess complained. She clapped her hand over her eyes. "I can't watch."

Nancy kept one eye open, one eye closed. After three trumpet blasts the knights began to charge. George jumped to her feet and began to cheer, "Sir Mayor the Strong is red hot! Sir Bragalot is all shot!"

Nancy gasped as the knights' lances clashed. Sir Bragalot knocked the mayor's lance from his hand—and the mayor from his horse!

The whole crowd jumped to its feet as Mayor Strong lay motionless on the ground. Just when Nancy thought the mayor was hurt, he jumped up, raised his visor, and grinned.

"I think I'll stick to being the mayor of River Heights!" Mayor Strong boomed.

The cheering was so loud that the bleachers shook. Sir Mayor the Strong and Sir Bragalot took off their gloves and shook hands. Then Seth led the horses away from the field.

"I want to follow Speckle," Nancy said, standing up, "and see if he's really Sparkle."

The girls left the jousting field. They found the horses inside a pen behind the grandstand. Both were nibbling hay off the ground.

"They're still wearing their blankets and headdresses," Bess said, peering through the chain-link fence. "Now we can't see if Speckle has a horn or not."

"Who says we can't?" George asked. She reached over the gate, lifted the latch, and swung it open.

"George, we're not allowed in there," Nancy called.

"This is a medieval festival!" Bess cried. "If they have a jousting field, they probably have a dungeon, too."

But George was already inside the horse pen.

"Do you want to see if Speckle is Sparkle or not?" she demanded.

To Nancy the answer was yes. She darted into the pen, followed by a groaning Bess. George ran straight to Speckle and tugged gently on his headdress.

"This thing is strapped on tight," George said. "He'll never hold still enough for us to look underneath."

"When Chip won't hold still for her bath, I pet her gently," Nancy said. "If it works with dogs, maybe it works with horses—or unicorns."

Nancy walked to Speckle's side, careful not to get swatted by his tail. She lifted the horsy-smelling blanket. She was about to pet Speckle when her hand froze.

"Bess, George," Nancy called. "I think I know why they call him Speckle."

"Why?" Bess asked as she and George ran over.

Nancy pointed to a flurry of black speckles on Speckle's coat. "Because of these," she said.

"Sparkle had no speckles," Bess sighed.

"So Speckle isn't Sparkle," George decided.

"Which means," Nancy said, letting the horse blanket drop over Speckle's back, "he's a horse and not a unicorn."

"You again?" a voice shouted. "Get out of there. It's not safe!"

Nancy gulped as they spun around. Glaring at them from outside the fence was Seth.

"Don't throw us into the dungeon!" Bess pleaded. "We have a spelling bee in a few weeks! And our book reports are due next Friday and—"

"Aren't you those girls who were in Sparkle's pen yesterday?" Seth cut in. "What do you want with Speckle?"

"Nothing anymore," George said.

But Nancy still had questions. "What were you helping the mayor with yesterday?" she asked Seth. "When you should have been watching Sparkle?"

"I was giving the mayor a riding lesson," Seth said. "And as you just saw, he needed a lot more than just one."

Seth held the gate open as Nancy, Bess, and George filed out of the pen.

"What do you think happened to Sparkle the unicorn, Seth?" Bess asked.

"Who knows?" Seth groaned. "But if he doesn't show up soon, Rex is going to flip."

As the girls walked away from the pen, Nancy glanced at her watch. Destiny's party would start in about an hour. They had to figure out a way to get to it.

"You guys," George said, "check it out!"

Nancy looked up from her watch. George was pointing to a huge open tent filled with racks of wizard robes, jester caps, and crowns—even a suit of armor. The costumes were great, and they gave Nancy an idea!

"Destiny is having a medieval party, right?" Nancy asked. "So everyone will be wearing medieval costumes, right?"

"Right!" Bess and George said together.

The girls raced into the tent. Two women dressed in long skirts and puffy-sleeved blouses were hanging up long capes. Their name tags read LADY SUE and LADY INEZ.

"May we borrow some costumes, please?" Nancy asked.

"Borrow?" Lady Sue chuckled.

"This isn't a library, kids," Lady Inez said. "Everything in here is for sale."

The girls traded disappointed looks. They didn't have enough money to buy costumes. But just as they were about to leave, Lady Sue called out, "Hey, wait! Aren't you Louise Fayne's daughter?"

"Who, me?" George asked, turning around.

"You were with your mom at the staff meeting," Lady Inez said. "You helped cut her delicious pies and cakes."

"That was me," George agreed.

"Your mom always gives us free food here," Lady Sue said with a warm smile. "So we'll let you borrow some costumes—for free."

Lady Sue and Lady Inez helped the girls pick out perfect costumes. Nancy chose a purple velvet gown with black trim. After trying on five dresses, Bess decided on a long pink skirt and a white blouse embroidered with pink flowers. George refused to wear a long dress or skirt. Instead, she chose an orange tunic with dark green tights.

"We may have costumes," George said as they left the tent, "but we don't have invitations to Destiny's party."

"What if her parents don't let us inside?" Bess asked.

"We don't have to go inside the house," Nancy explained. "If Destiny has Sparkle, she's probably keeping him in the backyard."

The girls were carrying their regular clothes when they saw two friends from school, Marcy Ruben and Kendra Jackson. They'd just had their faces painted to look like cats, with colorful whiskers.

"Meow!" Kendra howled, swiping a pretend paw.

Nancy giggled. Their faces were funny. But

even funnier were the necklaces they were wearing: tiny clear plastic bottles hanging from black cords. Packed inside the bottles were wispy white hairs.

"What's that?" Nancy asked, nodding at the bottles.

"They're good luck charms," Kendra said. "Toby Leo is selling them."

"Toby?" Nancy asked.

Marcy pointed to Toby walking past a candy apple stall. In his hands was a medium-size cardboard box.

"Get your unicorn hair right here," Toby was yelling as he walked. "Guaranteed to bring you good luck!"

"Bess, George!" Nancy exclaimed. "Did he just say *unicorn* hair?"

chaPTeR Six

Happy Birthday to Clue!

"Hey, Toby!" George shouted. "Where did you get the unicorn hair?"

"Du-uh!" Toby shouted back. "From a unicorn!"

"Can we see it, please?" Nancy asked, stepping

forward. But Toby spun on his heel and took off running.

"Get him!" George shouted. She dropped the bundle of clothes she was holding and chased Toby.

"I'm not dropping my clothes on the dirty ground!" Bess cried.

Neither would Nancy. So with bundles in their arms Nancy and Bess joined George in the chase. They didn't get very far as their long skirts tangled around their ankles.

"Whoa!" Nancy cried as she tripped and fell.

"Ow!" Bess screamed as she tumbled to the ground.

George stopped running. Groaning under her breath, she ran back to help her friends up.

"Our hands were full," Bess complained. "We couldn't hold up our long skirts."

"I told you to wear a tunic and tights instead," George said, and groaned. "Now Toby got away!"

"At least we know he has unicorn hair," Nancy said. "And there's only one unicorn we know."

"Sparkle," Bess declared.

While Nancy and Bess dusted themselves off, Mrs. Fayne walked over.

"Do you like our clothes, Aunt Louise?" Bess asked, twirling around. "Lady Sue and Lady Inez let us borrow them for free."

"How nice of them," Mrs. Fayne said. She wiggled her car keys in her hand. "I have to go back to the house to pick up some pies. Want to come with me?"

Nancy smiled to herself. This was their big chance!

"The birthday party," Nancy whispered to her friends.

"Oh, right," George whispered back. She smiled at her mother and said, "Mom, can you please drop us off at Destiny Delgado's house on the way? We want to wish her a happy birthday."

"And look for some clues along the way," Nancy said superquickly so they wouldn't be lying.

"I once catered a party at the Delgados', so I know where they live," Mrs. Fayne said. "But do you have invitations for Destiny's party?"

The girls exchanged worried looks. There it was. The *I* word.

"Um, not exactly, Mrs. Fayne," Nancy said. "But if you drop us off and pick us up on your way back to the fair, we'll have enough time to say happy birthday and won't stay too long."

"Okay, then," Mrs. Fayne said with a nod.

"Yippee!" Bess cheered with a little hop.

The girls followed Mrs. Fayne to the van. Nancy and Bess carefully lifted their skirts to climb into the backseat. George jumped in after them.

"If we don't find Sparkle at Destiny's house, we'll look for Toby later," Nancy said.

"When we're all wearing *pants*!" George declared.

Mrs. Fayne drove the short distance to Destiny's. Nancy had seen the house before, so she knew what to expect: a mansion.

After checking out the fountain in the front yard, filled with real fish, Mrs. Fayne rang the doorbell. Instead of *ding-dong* it played the tune "Happy Birthday to You."

"How did they do that?" George whispered.

"Well, hello!" Mrs. Delgado said as she opened the door. She smiled at Mrs. Fayne. "Oh . . . we're not using your catering service today."

"Yes, I know, but I'm not here to deliver food," Mrs. Fayne said, forcing a smile. "My daughter and her friends would like to wish Destiny a happy birthday."

Mrs. Delgado looked the girls up and down. She then smiled and said, "And they're dressed for the party too!"

Bess spread out her skirt and curtsied.

"Why don't you go around to the backyard?" Mrs. Delgado said. "That's where Princess Destiny is holding court."

"Have fun, girls," Mrs. Fayne said. "See you soon."

"Are we lucky or what?" George whispered as they scurried around the house. They froze when the backyard came into view.

"Ohmigosh!" Bess squeaked. "It looks like a mini Dragon's Breath Fair!"

Nancy couldn't believe it either. On the neatly trimmed lawn stood a miniature wooden castle—big enough for at least ten kids to step inside! Instead of balloons there were banners hanging from trees. Sticking straight up from the ground was a maypole with colorful ribbons blowing in the breeze. Sitting around the maypole were Destiny and her guests—all dressed in medieval costumes.

"She's opening her presents," Nancy whispered.

After ripping open a package, Destiny dropped the wrapping paper onto the grass.

"Oooh!" Destiny swooned as she held up a laptop computer. "Now I have one in hot pink."

While her guests oohed and ahhed, the girls glanced around the yard.

"No unicorn sighting," Nancy whispered.

"That castle is big enough for Sparkle," Bess whispered. "Maybe Destiny is keeping him in there."

The girls waited for Destiny to open the next big gift. Then, when all eyes were on the birthday girl, the Clue Crew scurried toward the castle.

As they hid behind it, Nancy heard bumping sounds coming from inside.

"Someone is in there," Nancy whispered.

"Someone or something," George whispered.

"It's probably Sparkle trying to break down the walls with his horn!" Bess said.

"Don't worry, Sparkle!" George called through the castle wall. "We'll save you!"

The girls ran around the castle to the door. George grabbed the handle and gave it a yank. The door swung open and—

"ROOOOOOAAAARRRRR!"

Nancy, Bess, and George jumped back as a giant green head popped out of the door. Inside its huge gaping mouth were two rows of needle-sharp teeth!

"That is no unicorn!" George shouted. "That's a *dragon*!"

CHAPTER SEVEN

Things Get Hairy

Bess screamed as the gigantic dragon head jerked forward. By now Destiny and her guests were racing over.

"Run, Destiny!" Bess warned. "Dragons carry off princesses—and you're the biggest princess we know!"

Instead of running, Destiny stepped right up to the dragon. She looked him straight in his bulging eyes and said, "You're too early. You were supposed to come out and pretend to light the candles on my cake with your dragon breath. Now the joke is ruined, Daddy."

"Daddy?" Nancy whispered to Bess and George.

The dragon's claws reached up to pull off its

giant head. Underneath was the red, sweaty face of Mr. Delgado!

So that's what that noise was, Nancy thought, feeling dumb. *His mask bumping against the wall.*

"Sorry, sweetie," Mr. Delgado said. He nodded at Nancy, Bess, and George. "But your friends here opened the door. I thought that was my cue to jump out and roar."

Destiny stared at Nancy, Bess, and George. Then she shook her head and said, "Those aren't my friends. I never invited them!"

"Uh-oh," George muttered.

"They're from our school," a boy dressed as a medieval baker said. "I think they're in third grade."

"Wait a minute," Destiny said as she circled Nancy, Bess, and George. "I think I know who you are. You're those detectives, aren't you?"

"We're the Clue Crew," Bess said with a smile. "And we're solving the mystery of the missing unicorn. We think you stole him because— OWWWW!"

Nancy jabbed Bess with her elbow. She didn't want to embarrass Destiny in front of her father and friends. But it was too late.

"Is that why you crashed my party?" Destiny demanded.

"We didn't really crash," Nancy said quickly. "Your mom invited us in so we could say happy birthday."

"Happy birthday!" Nancy, Bess, and George said at the same time.

"Everything is fine, princess," Mr. Delgado said. "Why don't you go back to your party and have a tubular time?"

"Not until these *spies* leave!" Destiny blurted.

"Not until you tell us where you were during the parade when Sparkle went missing!" George blurted at the same time.

"The parade?" Destiny said. "I was *in* the parade!"

"You were?" Nancy asked.

"When I couldn't get the unicorn for my party, Rex invited me to sit on the princess float,"

Destiny said. She jutted her chin into the air. "Didn't you see me?"

Bess and George shook their heads. Nancy didn't remember seeing Destiny in the parade either. But she did remember something else.

"We left the parade to look for my wand," Nancy whispered to her friends. "We probably missed the princess float."

A sudden trumpet blast made everyone jump.

"My cake!" Destiny squealed, jumping up and down. "My cake is coming! My cake is coming!"

Destiny and her friends stampeded past the girls, almost knocking them down.

"You can have some cake too, girls," Mr. Delgado said. He pulled the mask over his head. "Now, if you'll excuse me—it's showtime!"

A cake shaped like a castle was wheeled into the yard by two boys dressed as knights. Nancy recognized one of the knights as they stepped away from the cake. It was Ned Nickerson, her friend from school.

"Don't ask," Ned groaned to Nancy. "My

parents are friends with Destiny's parents. I had to do it."

Everyone laughed as Mr. Delgado pretended to light the candles with his dragon's breath. He finally pulled off his mask and lit the candles with a match.

"My mom could have baked that cake with her eyes closed," George muttered.

"Let's go," Nancy said.

"But we didn't have cake yet," Bess protested. "And we didn't get our goody bags—"

"We're not getting goody bags," Nancy interrupted. "And who wants gray cake, anyway?"

They were about to leave when Nancy felt someone tap her shoulder. A girl dressed in a long green gown was standing behind her.

"I'm Sophie Wang," the girl said quickly.

"You mean the Sophie who called me yesterday?" Nancy asked, surprised. "Did they find your horse, Carrot Cake?"

"No," Sophie said with a frown. "I had to practice with Babe this morning at the riding academy."

"You mean the horse with oat breath?" Nancy asked.

Sophie nodded sadly. "They're still not telling me what happened to Carrot Cake," she said. "I can't believe you'd rather look for a unicorn than a missing horse. Everybody knows there's no such thing as unicorns."

"There is too!" Bess said. "We saw one with our own eyes."

"George, your mom is here to pick you up," Mrs. Delgado called to them.

Nancy felt bad for Sophie. But as long as

Sparkle was still missing, they couldn't look for Carrot Cake.

"Sorry, Sophie," Nancy said. "We've got to go."

The girls rode in Mrs. Fayne's van back to the Dragon's Breath Fair. Nancy tried not to think about Sophie and how sad she'd looked.

"How do we know Destiny was telling the truth about the parade?" George asked.

"We don't," Nancy said. "That's why we have to find someone who would know for sure. Someone like Rex."

After the van arrived at the fairgrounds, the girls jumped out. First they helped Mrs. Fayne unload pie boxes. Next they ran to look for Rex. They found him eating a pretzel as he strolled past the game stalls.

"Mr. Martindale, Mr. Martindale!" Nancy called as they ran to him. "Was Destiny Delgado on the princess float?"

"Destiny?" Rex sputtered pretzel crumbs. "It wasn't enough for Destiny to be a princess. She had to be queen!"

Nancy raised an eyebrow at Bess and George. That proved Destiny had been on the float. But what about her dad?

"Do you know where Destiny's father was?" Nancy asked.

"On the float too." Rex groaned. "He wanted to make sure everybody cheered for Destiny."

"So Destiny was telling the truth," Bess said.

Rex looked confused. He gave his head a shake and said, "If you'll excuse me, I have a mud-wrestling contest to introduce."

"Wait, please," Nancy said. "What about Sparkle the unicorn? Did you tell the police that he's missing yet?"

Rex froze at the mention of Sparkle . . . or at the mention of the police!

"No," Rex said. "I'll handle it myself."

Nancy, Bess, and George watched Rex hurry off.

"Did you see that?" George asked. "When we asked Rex about the police, he practically flipped."

"But he did help us rule out Destiny," Nancy said. "Now our only suspect is Toby."

The girls looked around the fairgrounds for Toby. Instead, they found Toby's best friend, Peter Patino. Peter was standing in the line for giant turkey drumsticks.

"Hi, Peter," Nancy said as they walked over.

"Hey," Peter said, nodding toward the stall. "Did you see the size of those things? Turkeys must have been huge in medieval times!"

"Peter, have you seen Toby around?" Nancy asked.

"He was just here, but he went back home," Peter said. "He said he ran out of unicorn hair and had to get more."

"More?" Nancy gasped.

The girls backed away from Peter. They were too stunned to even thank him for the information.

"If Toby is getting more unicorn hair," Nancy said, "it means he's cutting Sparkle's beautiful mane and tail!"

The girls ran to Mrs. Fayne. But when they asked her to please drive them to Toby's house, she shook her head.

"I was just about to drive us all home," Mrs. Fayne said. "The fair is closing in less than an hour."

Nancy turned to her friends and said, "Don't worry. We'll find Toby first thing in the morning."

"By then Sparkle will be bald!" Bess cried.

"At least we know Toby has Sparkle," George said. "I wonder if the kids who bought his hair had any luck."

"If they did, then we'll know Sparkle is a unicorn for sure," Bess said with a little smile.

After helping the vendors clean up, Mrs. Fayne drove the girls home. She dropped Nancy off at her house first. Hannah was waiting on the doorstep with Chocolate Chip. She usually welcomed Nancy with a cheery smile, but not today.

"My vegetable garden was ruined today," Hannah said, and sighed.

"No way!" Nancy gasped. Chip followed her as she ran around to the back of the house. Her father was in the backyard, standing over a few straggly stalks.

"It's a shame," Mr. Drew said with a frown. "Hannah's carrots and tomatoes totally disappeared."

"Disappeared?" Nancy asked. She turned to stare at her magic wand, which was still on the picnic table. The glittery star was pointed straight at the garden!

Oh no, Nancy thought. *Did I make the vegetable garden disappear too?*

ChAPTER EigHT

Vanishing Veggies

"Don't look so worried, Nancy," Mr. Drew said with a smile. "Chip probably got a little hungry, that's all."

"It wasn't Chip," Hannah said. "I took Chip to the groomer today. The garden was like this when we got back."

"It must have been a hungry deer, then," Mr. Drew said. "We're not too far away from the woods."

"At least someone likes veggies," Hannah said, tossing Nancy a wink.

"I like veggies, Hannah!" Nancy said, trying to smile. What she didn't like was her new wand. It may not have made Sparkle disappear, but when it came to Hannah's veggie garden, it seemed to be guilty.

That does it, Nancy decided, eyeing the wand on the table. *That thing goes back tomorrow!*

"You're bringing your wand to the festival today?" Hannah asked Nancy the next morning.

Nancy slipped the purple and silver wand into her backpack, careful not to point it at herself.

"I'm returning it, Hannah," Nancy said. "I don't like the color."

"But purple is your favorite," Hannah said.

"Um . . . I've got to go now, Hannah," Nancy said. She opened the door. "Bess and George are waiting outside."

Nancy blew Hannah a kiss, then ran out the door. She didn't mention the wand to Bess and George as she joined them on the sidewalk.

All three girls were wearing their medieval costumes again that morning.

"I hope we don't have to do any running today," Bess said, nodding down at her long skirt.

"How did girls do anything in those days?"

"They probably never did cartwheels," George said, sighing. "Boy, am I glad it's the twenty-first century!"

"Me too," Nancy agreed. She looked from George to Bess. "Did anyone find Toby Leo's address last night?"

"Got it!" George said. "Toby lives on Minnow Street, four blocks away. That means we can walk there before my mom picks us up."

"Sweet!" Bess said.

Nancy, Bess, and George all had the same rules. They could walk up to five blocks from their houses as long as they were together.

Nancy and Bess lifted the hems of their skirts as they headed to Minnow Street. They found the Leo house in the middle of the block. They also found a mob of kids yelling: "We want our money back! We want our money back!"

The girls walked over to Shelby Metcalf from their class. Shelby was the loudest yeller in the crowd.

"What's up, Shelby?" George asked.

"Toby promised his unicorn hair was good luck," Shelby yelled into George's face. "And all we had was *bad* luck!"

"Yeah!" Quincy Taylor said. "I found out my grandma is moving into my room—and she snores!"

"And I tripped in ballet last night!" Nadine Nardo cried. "During my recital. If that isn't bad luck, what is?"

The girls stepped back as the kids kept shouting.

"If they all had *bad* luck," Bess shouted above the noise, "does that mean Sparkle isn't a real unicorn?"

"No one ever said unicorn hair was lucky," George said with a shrug. "Just the whole unicorn."

A window suddenly flew up. Toby stuck his head out and yelled, "Get lost or I'll call my dog. And you don't want to mess with him!"

Nancy wanted to giggle. Duncan the sheepdog with his long shaggy hair was a big friendly mush. But the kids walked away, grumbling.

"What do *you* want?" Toby called down to the girls.

"We want to know where you got all that unicorn hair!" Nancy shouted up. "The ones you sold to those kids."

"None of your beeswax!" Toby shouted back.

"Yes, it is!" Nancy insisted. "Sparkle the unicorn went missing from the Dragon's Breath Fair on Friday. Did you steal him for his lucky hair?"

"Or unlucky!" George added.

"I didn't steal any unicorn," Toby said.

Bess pulled the tiny bell from her pocket. She jingled it in the air and said, "How do you explain this bell I found in Sparkle's pen?" she asked. "Wasn't it part of your jester's cap?"

Instead of answering, Toby whistled loudly. Then he shut his window with a bang.

"Let's check the backyard," Nancy said. "If Toby has Sparkle, he's probably there."

The girls began rounding the house. But as

they were about to enter the backyard—

"WOOOOF!"

Nancy froze as a huge white creature bounded out from behind the house. But it wasn't Sparkle the unicorn. It was Duncan the sheepdog!

Bess shrieked as Duncan knocked her to the ground with his huge paws. She shrieked even louder as Duncan began licking her face.

"Ewww! Dog spit!" Bess cried. "Get him off!"

Nancy grabbed for Duncan's collar. But he was wearing a bandana around his neck instead.

"Come on, boy," Nancy said, gently tugging his bandana. "Bess doesn't like dog spit."

"And you do?" Bess cried, standing up.

George tilted her head as she studied Duncan. "What happened to all his white shaggy hair?" she asked.

"He must have gotten a haircut," Nancy said. But as she pet Duncan, she noticed something about his bandana. It was polka-dotted—the exact same bandanna Chip was wearing from *her* groomer!

"Wait a minute," Nancy said. "I think I know where Toby got those hairs. And they weren't from a unicorn."

"You mean that hairy stuff in the jar belonged to Duncan?" Bess asked.

"If Duncan was at the Jet Set Pet," Nancy explained, "Toby probably asked the groomer for some of his hair."

"Okay, Clue Crew, so you figured it out!" Toby yelled from his window, open again. "Now can you please keep your big mouths shut?"

"We won't tell the kids that you sold them dog hair," Nancy shouted up. "That's your job."

"So is giving them their money back," George said.

"Can't!" Toby said. "I already spent it at the

71

Dragon's Breath Fair. Mostly on caramel apples with nuts."

"My favorite," Bess said, licking her lips.

"Mine too, until I ate seven of them!" Toby groaned. He then gagged, clapped his hand over his mouth, and shot away from the window.

"I don't think he's got Sparkle," Nancy decided.

"And I don't think caramel candy apples are my favorite anymore," Bess said, and sighed.

"But how does that explain the bell Bess found in Sparkle's pen?" George asked. "Toby *was* wearing bells!"

As the girls left the yard, they passed the Leos' family car. Nancy glanced into the backseat. She spotted Toby's jester costume and cap draped over the front seat. It was covered with plastic from the cleaners. Nancy pressed her nose against the window to study the costume.

"Aha," Nancy said.

"Aha what?" George asked.

"The bell Bess found in Sparkle's pen was golden," Nancy said. She pointed at the cap inside the car. "The bells on Toby's cap are silver."

"Then who did that bell belong to?" George wondered.

Nancy, Bess, and George waited on the sidewalk until Mrs. Fayne picked them up and drove them to the fair.

"We have one more day to look for clues," Nancy said as they climbed out of the van. "But before we do that, I have to do something very important."

Bess and George followed Nancy to Enchanted Elly's tent. There she pulled the pretty purple magic wand out of her backpack.

"I want to return this, please," Nancy told Elly. "You don't have to give me my money back."

Bess and George looked surprised. Elly just chuckled and said, "What's the matter? Didn't get your gown for the prince's ball?"

Nancy looked away from Elly. How could she tell her that the wand might have made a vegetable garden disappear? And maybe even a unicorn?

"Elly, do you know how to catch a unicorn?"

Bess asked, interrupting Nancy's thoughts.

"A unicorn!" Elly declared. "Unicorns love the woods. You might catch one there."

"Or poison ivy," George mumbled as the girls left.

"Why did you return the wand, Nancy?" Bess asked. "Are you beginning to think you made Sparkle disappear?"

Nancy looked at Bess. So far they hadn't found Sparkle—anywhere. But she refused to give up.

"Let's go back to Sparkle's pen," Nancy said. "Maybe we can find more clues."

On the way the girls passed a man juggling fire, an archery contest, and a cart where someone was selling peanuts. But when they passed a horse stable, they had to stop.

"I'll bet these horses are for the jousts!" George said as they entered the stable.

"There's Speckle!" Bess said, pointing to a white horse with black speckles.

Nancy studied the horses, their big handsome heads hanging over the stall doors.

"You know," Nancy said, half to herself, "those horses look like unicorns without the horns."

"Are you saying Sparkle was a *horse*?" Bess asked.

Nancy noticed a list hanging on the stable wall. It was a list of the horses and what to feed them. She read the names out loud: "Speckle, Midnight, Darby, Thunderfoot, Lindy—Ohmigosh!"

"Ohmigosh?" Bess giggled. "That's a weird name for a horse."

"No!" Nancy said. "Look at the last name on the list."

Bess and George looked up too. Then their mouths dropped wide open. Speckle was the first name on the list. But the last name was *Sparkle*!

CHAPTER NINE

Swingy Thingy

"Not only is Sparkle on the list," George pointed out, "he ate the same stuff the other horses ate. Vegetables."

Vegetables? The word hit Nancy like a ton of cauliflower.

"Someone ate vegetables from Hannah's garden yesterday," Nancy said.

"Carrots from my neighbors' garden were nibbled on too," Bess said. "It happened Friday during the night."

Nancy stared at Bess. Hannah's garden wasn't the only garden that had been nibbled on. So that meant one thing. . . .

"That's great!" Nancy exclaimed.

"What's so great about trashed gardens?" George asked.

"Not about the gardens—about my wand," Nancy explained. "It wasn't anywhere near Bess's neighbors' garden, so it couldn't have made the veggies disappear."

"Huh?" Bess asked.

"My dad thought deer had eaten the veggies," Nancy explained. "Now I think it was Sparkle— the horse!"

"But Sparkle has a *horn*!" Bess said.

"We never saw Sparkle up close," Nancy said. "His horn could have been fake."

"Oh, phooey!" Bess complained. "We finally see a real unicorn and he's not even for real."

"Well, now that we think Sparkle is a horse," Nancy asked, "how do we catch him?"

Bess tapped her chin as she seemed to think about it. Her eyes finally lit up, and she said, "Follow me!"

Nancy and George followed Bess as she collected carrots from Seth, string from Mrs. Fayne's cake boxes, and a coat hanger from Lady Sue and Lady Inez's costume tent. In less than an hour Bess had built a new gadget.

"Ta-daa!" Bess sang. She held up her carrot mobile.

"How does it work?" Nancy asked.

"If Sparkle likes carrots," Bess explained, "we hang it in the woods and wait until he gets a snack attack."

The girls weren't allowed into the real woods, so they hung the carrot mobile in the Wizardly Woods instead.

George gave Bess a boost so she could hook the mobile onto the branch of a tree.

There was nothing to do now but wait.

"NEEEEEEEEEYYYYYY!"

Nancy, Bess, and George froze.

"Did you just hear what I just heard?" Nancy asked.

The girls turned and walked a few feet into the woods.

There, munching on the carrots, was a horse. A big beautiful white horse!

"It's Sparkle!" Nancy whispered.

CHAPTER TEN

Horse? Of Course!

"He still has a silver horn in the middle of his forehead," Bess whispered.

Sparkle kept munching as the girls stepped closer. Nancy gently touched the horn. It felt like cardboard. And silver glitter came off on her hand.

"It's not real," Nancy confirmed.

George tugged at an elastic band under Sparkle's mane that connected the horn to his forehead. "Tacky, tacky, tacky," she said. "I wear better costumes on Halloween!"

"But look at this," Bess said. She pointed to a delicate collar around Sparkle's neck. It was decorated with tiny golden bells. "No wonder I found a bell inside his pen."

"The main thing is that we found Sparkle," Nancy exclaimed, petting the horse's fluffy white mane.

"Now that we've found Sparkle the horse," George said, "how do we get him back to the fair?"

"Like this," Bess answered. She pulled a carrot off the mobile and held it up. "Sparkle, forward march!"

Sparkle followed the girls out of the woods while Bess waved the carrot high in the air. As they made their way through the fairgrounds, people stopped to point.

Rex ran toward Sparkle, a huge smile on his face.

"Huzzah, good people!" Rex shouted. "Our unicorn has returned to the Dragon's Breath Fair!"

Nancy and her friends stopped walking. Sparkle was happy to nibble on the carrot, still in Bess's hand.

"You mean *horse*, Mr. Martindale," Nancy corrected.

"H-h-horse?" Rex stammered.

"A poor hungry horse who had to eat veggies from people's gardens because he couldn't find his way home," Bess added.

Rex whisked the girls away from the crowd. "Ix-nay on the orse-hay, will you, kids?" he hissed.

Nancy frowned. Rex still wanted to keep the secret of the unicorn. But this was one secret Nancy refused to keep.

"Sorry, Mr. Martindale," Nancy said. "But why didn't you tell Police Chief McGinnis that Sparkle was missing?"

Rex's eyes darted from side to side. Then he took a deep breath and said, "Look, I didn't tell the police because they would have called the River Heights Riding Academy!"

"The River Heights Riding Academy?" Nancy repeated. "What do they have to do with Sparkle?"

"That's where I borrowed Sparkle from," Rex explained. "I needed a white horse to disguise as a unicorn."

"And they gave him to you?" George asked. She snapped her fingers. "Just like that?"

"My friend Matt works at the riding academy," Rex explained. "He said I could borrow the horse for the fair as long as I promised to take good care of him."

"So if Matt had found out you'd lost Sparkle, he'd know you goofed, right?" Bess asked.

"Right," Rex sighed.

Nancy watched Rex nod his head. He looked so sad that it seemed the feather in his cap practically drooped. But there was something about his story that sounded familiar. Matt . . . River Heights Riding Academy . . . Where had she heard all that before?

"NEEEEEEEYYYYYYYY!" Sparkle suddenly whinnied.

Everyone gasped as the white horse shot off and galloped across the fairgrounds.

"Get him!" Rex cried. "We can't lose him again!"

Bess lifted the hem of her skirt and groaned, "Here we go again!"

Rex and the girls chased Sparkle past the food and game stalls. Sparkle's belled collar jangled as he headed straight toward his pen.

Standing near the pen was Seth. The moment he saw the charging horse, his jaw dropped.

"Open the gate, Seth! Open the gate!" Rex shouted.

But before Seth reached the gate, Sparkle took a flying leap over the fence.

"Wow!" George gasped. "Did you see that?"

Everyone watched as Sparkle trotted over to a pile of hay and began to eat.

"I never saw a horse jump that high!" Seth exclaimed.

"So that's how Sparkle got out of his pen," Nancy said excitedly. "He jumped over the fence!"

While Rex and Seth entered the pen through the gate, the girls traded big high fives.

"Good work, Clue Crew!" Nancy said. "We solved the case of the missing unicorn that turned out to be a missing horse!"

"Thanks to Bess's carrot mobile," George declared.

"A piece of cake!" Bess said, flapping her hand.

Carrot . . . Cake? Nancy grinned as everything else fell into place. The River Heights Riding Academy . . . Matt the instructor . . . Sophie Wang.

"You guys," Nancy said, "I think I know the horse's real name. And it isn't Sparkle!"

"Go, Carrot Cake!" Nancy cheered.

It was a week after the Dragon's Breath Fair. Nancy, Bess, and George were having a great time watching the River Heights Riding Academy horse show.

Nancy waved her wand as she cheered. It was

the same beautiful wand she had gotten back from Enchanted Elly before the fair had ended. It had never been magical, but it was still pretty.

The girls cheered for Sophie as she jumped Carrot Cake over a row of fences. Nancy remembered Sophie's shock when they'd told her about Carrot Cake.

"Are you sure it's Carrot Cake?" Sophie had asked.

"Totally," Nancy had assured her.

"He really was lost, but we found him!" Bess had said.

"But why didn't Matt just tell me he'd lent Carrot Cake to the Dragon's Breath Fair?" Sophie had asked.

"Rex wanted the unicorn to be a secret," Nancy had explained. "He probably told Matt to keep the secret too."

"The most important thing is that Carrot Cake is safe and back in time for the show," Sophie had said. "I knew you guys were good."

Sophie had said thanks by giving Nancy, Bess, and George tickets to the horse show that coming Saturday.

"I think I'm going to eat more carrots from now on," George said as Sophie rode around the ring. "If they can make Carrot Cake jump like that, think of what it can do for me when I play basketball."

"Nancy," Bess asked with a dreamy look on her face, "do you think we'll ever see a leaping unicorn?"

Nancy watched as Carrot Cake jumped over the highest fence in the ring.

"We just saw a flying horse," Nancy said excitedly. "So *anything* is possible!"

Make a magic wand!

Wishing you could have a beautiful wand just like Nancy's? *And so you shall!*

You Will Need:
A stick, chopstick, or plastic drinking straw
A pen or pencil
Sturdy cardboard
Scissors
Glue
Sparkly glitter
Clear tape
Strips of colorful ribbons

Let the magic begin!

❀ Draw a star on the cardboard.

❀ Carefully cut the star out.

❀ Cover one side of the star with glue.

✿ While glue is still wet, sprinkle glitter all over star.

✿ After one side of your star is dry, flip over and glue and put glitter on the other side.

✿ When glue and glitter have completely dried, attach star to the top of the stick, chopstick, or straw with clear tape.

✿ Tie colorful ribbons to the stick right under the star, letting the ends stream down.

✿ Now work your new wand!

Hint: Go wizard-wild by painting the stick your favorite color or by gluing beads, sequins, or feathers onto your star. And remember—your wand doesn't have to be magic to be totally *spellbinding*!

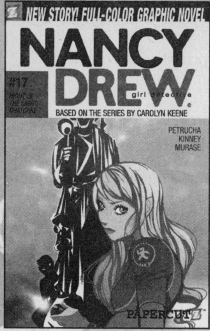